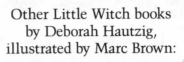

Other Little Witch books
by Deborah Hautzig,
illustrated by Marc Brown:

LITTLE WITCH'S BIG NIGHT
HAPPY BIRTHDAY, LITTLE WITCH

Little Witch's Book of Magic Spells

by
Deborah Hautzig

illustrated by
Marc Brown

Random House 🏠 New York

Little Witch lives in a haunted house with Mother Witch, her cat, Bow-Wow, and her bat, Scrubby. Mother Witch tries to teach Little Witch to scare people, cast wicked spells, and do other witchy things. But Little Witch can't help it...she is a good little witch who does nice things. And her mother loves her anyway! Here are some of her magic spells.

Twiggly, wiggly
Creepy tree,
Make a tree house
Just for me.

Yucky, mucky
Bowl of peas,
Turn to popcorn
If you please!

Slurping, burping
Squiggling snake,
Turn into
A birthday cake.

Yappy, snappy
Growling dog,
You will be
A friendly frog!

Squawky, talky
Pesky crow,
Change into
A gentle doe.

Ooky, spooky
Cloudy night,
Stars come out
And shine your light.